Find the Sequel to Deathrunes and Dragons here:

Under A Torn Moon

Book Two in the Songs of Serathur

Other books by William Collins

A Darker Shade of Sorcery

http://www.amazon.com/gp/product/B01A3L1PS6

Moonlight War- Act I

https://www.amazon.com/dp/B01HLGKL9U

Moonlight War- Act II

The Dawnvel Druids

Deathrunes and Dragons

Songs of Serathur Book One

Darkness smothered him. Cloth pressed against his eye sockets and sucked against his lips with every ragged breath. Sweat and spit caused the sack to cling to his face like a second skin.

Varity could see nothing, yet used every other sense to picture his surroundings.

Thick hands squeezed flesh tight as they dragged him, the manacles squeezed flesh tighter still, biting, slicing, slick with blood.

They'd taken him down off the camel, where his head and neck had snapped up and down a hundred times during the journey. The feel in the air was of an upcoming meteor cascade brewing, it would hit today.

They must've reached the outpost, the soldiers crowding around to lead him through the fort, like a prized pig.

He smelled fire and unwashed skin. Heard the constant clink of armour and rustle of leather. The soldiers who'd captured him had been careful not to say too much, even when he played unconscious, and the sack had been around him since the moment they trussed him up on the camel. Varity didn't know why they'd gone to all this bother. He'd always known the outpost's location.

A cheer went up as stone replaced the sand beneath his feet. The shouts and jeers taught him much. Dusk elves and trolladin alike were amongst the soldiers, alongside the orcs and humans that made up the bulk.

They'd probably brought him in to the main courtyard with all that crowing, and the fires he could hear crackling merrily. Roast aurochs roasted on spits, a griffin too. Above all the other senses, he could almost taste the arrogance. Not on all of them, many soldiers were bored or miserable, but others were looking forward to the slaughter, to quashing another rebellion.

Someone spat on him, someone else tried and missed. He was jerked away, yanked down a flight of steps and away from the searing sunlight.

*

For hours he sat in darkness, or maybe the room was brightly lit. The sack was still tied around his head, hard to breathe, but not so much that he'd gasp his last before they had their way with him. They must've taken him far beneath the castle, he'd definitely been hauled through a cave tunnel, ammonia wafting from dirt around him. It was silent here, no notion that an army was stationed above.

The manacles were still there, but chains thick with rust had been added to them. They snaked around his forearms, binding him to the iron chair. And so Varity waited, feeling the cuts about his wrists knit together now the manacles had stopped rubbing. His captors were aware he was a Shamadar, they knew he could heal. He was counting on them not knowing much else though.

Metal screamed as a heavy door grated open, two pairs of boots echoed off stone, the sack was ripped from his head.

Varity blinked against the light. Only a single gaslight globe dangled from the ceiling, yet that single, sickly neon glow was blinding after so much dark.

He was in the dungeons of Fort Dusthold. *What an original place for a torture chamber?* The stone walls were slick with human stains and spongy with mould. Dominga banners lay draped across the walls, failing to hide the cracks that infected the stone like spiderwebs. He smiled to see the ceiling had a metre-long crack above his head. *Perfect.*

A hanging censer filled with myrrh tried in vain to wash away the aroma of past agony that coated the room. A single table and wooden chair were the only furnishings,

other than the metal throne Varity was chained to.
Definitely a torture chamber, judging by the silver tray and
its implements upon the table. A upside down metal bowl
on the tray caught his eye. His supernaturally improved
hearing detected a faint growling from within. *What
creature could that be?*

"Finally, I feared you'd forgotten me," Varity drawled,
smirking up at the two who'd entered.

The smaller of the duo took the chair opposite him.

Ah, he's to be my torturer then. The other occupant
confirmed his suspicions by taking place by the heavy
door, armed in burnished bronze armour and a dark blue
cloak.

For the first time since his capture, Varity felt a worm of
fear. He hadn't counted on his guard being so impressive.
He was a Ghunlin, his body vaguely humanoid, though his

flesh was coated in amber, and his head was that of an ant. Ghunlin were usually well under six feet though, and scrawnier than city beggars. The guard, however, was a Ghunlin Champion; a Ghunlin warrior species who stood ten-foot-tall, each of his mandibles long and sharp as daggers.

Varity's torturer was less impressive. He was slim even for a Mereshi, lank hair the shade of beetroot hung to his skeletal shoulders. The tiny white scales covering his body gave his flesh the resemblance of wax, broken only by the red gills either side of his throat. He wore faded brown breeches and a vest, both splattered with old blood. Velociraptor leather gloves went up to his elbows and edge of a faded slave brand peeked over one glove's lip.

So, he was one who'd rather join his oppressors than fight against them. Varity couldn't wholly blame him.

There was a damn-sight more chance of surviving under the Dominga's thumb then in attempting to pull them down.

"Thirsty yet?" The Mereshi growled.

"I could say the same for you. How long have you been out of water, friend?"

"We got a right funny one here," the Mereshi turned to the Ghunlin with a cackle. "Hours with that sack on his head and he still wants to play. Well, that just makes my job more fun." The amphibian turned back to Varity. "My name's Fellor. I like my patients to know who's treating them see, it's only polite."

"Your politeness is much appreciated."

Fellor's eye twitched. "I've had many like you, Shamadar. Many think they're hard to break--at first. They're always proven wrong."

"I'm already broken, just ask me what you want to know."

"Oh, it'll be that easy? That's no fun." The Mereshi's hand strayed to the tray of instruments, fingering a long silver tool, perhaps made to slide up one's nostril.

"Tell me, what brings one of your kind to war-ridden Cimhura in the first place?" Fellor leaned back in his chair, trying too hard to appear nonchalant. "Are you one of the many heroic fools flocking to Alentarcia to claim Arch Duke Ferdinez's reward. Word is he offered any fools from the guilds a huge reward to slay the Wendigo haunting his lands. I suppose he'd accept a Shamadar too."

"No, but that does sound like an intriguing opportunity. Thanks for the tip."

"You won't ever take another contract again, violet eyes." Fellor's nose wrinkled. "Carver scrape me, what is that awful stench, like garlic and triceratops dung.'

"The prisoner," the Ghunlin said between intermittent clicks, jerking his great head Varity's way.

"It's a highly regarded perfume actually, very popular in the Pastel Plains."

He disguised his relief that neither of them recognised the Filthworm blood he'd slathered on his neck and shirt before they'd captured him this morning.

Fellor looked down at him, smug satisfaction smeared across his face. He pulled a crinkled piece of parchment out of his pocket. "If being captured in ruins three miles away from our outpost wasn't proof enough of you scouting us, *this* was found in your cloak pocket. Don't try to deny it."

"Oh, that." Varity glanced at the paper, glimpsing words scrawled by his own hand on the page. "You'll never believe me, right, but I solemnly swear. I swear on the Carver himself, I just found that letter half-buried in the sands."

Fellor snorted. "It's written in Cimhuran swirls, lucky I can read their language, eh?" The Mereshi began to recite from the letter. "Please, child of ash. We beg your assistance. I know Shamadar are paid to hunt monsters, feral beasts and even stray mages, that your otherworldly gifts are to aid you in such endeavours. But we are desperate for aid. As a Shamadar, neutral to any wars, you can enter Fort Dusthold with immunity. If you would but go there, under the excuse of trade and shelter, we would be most gracious if you could report back the Dominga's numbers and weapons, and most importantly, any battle plans they are preparing for. My tribe offers you five-hundred-crescents for such information. The metal men of the Dominga are just as monstrous as those you must usually hunt. We hope you will accept our offer, since we heard you aided the Tusksplitter tribe in recent days."

Fellor finished reading and glared back at him. "Five-hundred-crescents eh? Was the gold worth your life?"

"I know, cheap, aren't I?" Varity chuckled.

"You will be crucified for this, ash-eater. But if you co-operate, I can make sure you'll get a nice, quick hanging instead. Why don't you save yourself the unnecessary agony?"

"Why do some people fixate on the ash thing?" Varity asked, as if speaking to himself. "Shamadar ingest just a little ash from a Shamharn statue to glean their power, and suddenly that's all anyone can focus on."

Fellor ignored him, instead returning to his smug, at-ease character. Varity could tell this fool was used to his patients being terrified of him before he touched a single instrument, but Varity would beat him at his own game.

"Quite the specimen, isn't he?" Fellor said to the Ghunlin, who merely clicked his mandibles incoherently.

"Pretty for a Shamadar, with those big violet eyes and rippling muscles. Most monster hunters I know have far more scars."

"Are you here to torture me, or come on to me?"

A second eye twitch. "I was merely expressing regret." Fellor leaned closer. "I can see the black rings surrounding those purple orbs. Does that come after you ingest that demonic ash?"

"It's one of the many symptoms." Varity sighed. "Inhuman strength, speed and healing make up for it though."

"Alas," said Fellor. "It's almost a shame to remove such lovely eyes."

"Maybe you could keep them and use them for the balls you lost when you joined the Dominga."

Fellor's expression curdled as he abandoned his act. "You Shamadar think you're untouchable, don't ya? Well, you might have the strength of seven men, but my Ghunlin associate has the strength of ten. And my Fengaul friend can heal from more grievous wounds than you after a few vitality transplants."

Transplants? Damn, did that mean the Dominga had a Leech-doctor at the outpost? That wasn't good at all.

Fellor's gills seemed to wiggle with mirth. "That's the thing with you monster slayers, you don't realise that as powerful as you are, there's always someone better."

"Same thing could be said for torturers."

Fellor lunged and struck with a backhanded blow. Varity laughed. Fellor struck again. And again.

"Quagging heljor," the Mereshi cursed after the fourth slap, shaking the sting out of his hand.

Varity smiled up his torturer, feeling a trickle of blood slither down his front teeth even as the tissue of his broken gums knitted themselves back together.

"Stop playing with him!" A new voice ordered. "A mere mortal like you won't hurt him with your soft flesh."

They all looked up as the door shut behind the newcomer. Varity's breath caught as he took her in. She stood six-feet-tall, just as broad and more thickly muscled than he was. Her blonde hair was pulled back into an elegant braid, emphasising the white horns gracing either side of her head. Her being a Fengaul barbarian was irrelevant, the fact the pale flesh of her bare arms was littered with scars that only runes could make was the problem.

The Ghunlin Champion was already simply big enough to be a problem, but the Runescrawler could undo everything.

Fellor looked incensed at being rebuked, yet there was fear there too. Of course, Fellor was right to fear her. Mages were more important than torturers after all, and meant a lot more to the Dominga.

"You don't know what you're in for do ya?" Fellor whirled back to him, snarling. Varity didn't know if the old fish-lover was angrier that his blows had little effect on Varity, or that he wasn't able to play his game with his newest patient.

"I'm somewhat familiar with the process actually. This isn't my first time being tortured. You're quite bad at it you know."

"But it will be your last." Fellor wrenched one of the implements off the table, a flaying knife. He seized Varity's wrist and twisted it over, pressing the knife against his inner arm. The steel was deathly cold, yet the pain it birthed would be hot as flame.

"Okay, okay," Varity cried, pretending to crumble. *Ah, acting. I've missed this. I can almost imagine being on stage again in front of hundreds.*

"Please…ask me anything. I'll talk…I'll talk."

Fellor's waxy face split into a rictus grin and he sat back on his chair, happy as an orc with the biggest tusks in his pack.

"The mouthy ones usually break first." Fellor told the barbarian woman. Varity wondered why he was trying to impress her so. *Maybe he's hoping to pass his torturer exam with flying colours?*

He abandoned the thought, remembering to keep his visage a tableau of terror.

"We already know many of the Cimhuran tribes are still loyal to the Dominga," said Fellor. "And we know of the three tribes who spearheaded this hopeless revolt. But there must be at least four more tribes aiding them." He held up the fake letter once again, brandishing it in front of Varity's face. "This letter proves you've worked for one rebel tribe already. You will tell us what treason you committed and the identity of the tribe who tasked you to spy on us."

Fellor pressed the flaying knife into Varity's arm, producing a bead of blood. "Start talking."

"Okay…the people from the letter was…the Tusksplitter tribe."

Confusion blanched across Fellor's face moments before rage dawned. "No, the letter says you already worked a contract for the Tusksplitters, you quagging fool. Which tribe are you working for now?"

Why haven't they reached the fort yet? He needed to buy more time, and he'd prefer not to bide that time in agony. He guessed he'd have to make up a tribe.

"Alright—please--don't!" He cried again as Fellor prepared to scrape his knife deep. "It's the Fangsmasher tribe. They're the ones you want."

"…Fangsmasher," Fellor mouthed, looking back at the barbarian sorceress. "Do we have that tribe on record?"

"He's playing you, fool," she snapped, glaring daggers at Varity.

Fellor's eye twitch turned into a spasm of fury barely kept at bay. "Fine. I see I'm gonna have to start chopping off fingers before we get anywhere. You Shamadar heal quick, but you can't grow back your toes, can ya? Or maybe I'll hack off an ear first."

"You're going about this all wrong." Varity purposely licked his lips and forced his eyes to dart around the room. Despite his less-than-optimum situation, it felt good to put be performing again. It had been years since he'd last enacted one of Churnpike's theatrical masterpieces. He missed it terribly What he would give to—*focus Varity!*

He slipped out of the fearful victim and back into the bored mercenary.

"I slay monsters, and occasionally miscreants, for money, right? You know I've also taken pay to aid these Cimhurans, which is against the Shamadar Legion's mandate. You should be appealing to my nature. I'm nothing more than a mercenary and like any good Paidblade, I'll turn on any employer for the right price. So, give me a better offer."

He smiled in a way he hoped a subtle nervousness would shine through.

Fellor snorted in disdain. "You expect us to *pay* you when we could rip the information from you for free?"

"Yes, but why get blood all over the floor? Listen, I know when I'm beaten. If you would but let me go and return the bag your men took from my person, I'll tell you all you want to know and then be on my merry way. It won't cost you nothing."

"Oh, this bag?" Fellor pulled a small sack from out of his cloak. He shook it, the jingle of jewels echoing throughout the room.

Just the one. Varity suppressed a grin.

"Did you kill a Jewelburner?" Fellor grunted, peering inside the bag.

"Careful," the barbarian said. "Don't let him touch one, in case he can burn it."

Fellor looked up at her in shock. "You reckon he's a Jewelburner as well as a Shamadar?"

She nodded. "The Shamadar Legion often recruits mages, they have a slightly better chance at surviving the ash. My soldiers removed any jewels he might have on him, just in case."

"Knowledge and beauty." Varity commended her. "And yes, one orcish brute ripped the very earrings from my innocent lobes. Highly unnecessary, I'm only looking to sell the jewels on."

"I reckon they're Dominga property now." Fellor sneered, tying the bag at his own belt.

"Enough," the barbarian woman snapped, her eyes, the yellow of pus-filled boils, locked onto his own. "You aren't getting anywhere, Fellor. I'm taking over."

"But Ranasta, Lord Raligant said I had hours to get the Shamadar to squeal." Fellor whined.

"We don't have hours," Ranasta snapped. "Out of the way."

She stalked forward with a leonine gait, Fellor scrambling away, surrendering his seat to her. He looked ready to spit fish eggs, but obeyed, with a murmured, "yes mistress."

Varity bestowed her with a dashing grin, saying nothing, but thinking rapidly. He knew she wouldn't be as easily manipulated as Fellor.

"May I say, you're exceptionally beautiful for a Leech-doctor, though I've met fiercer barbarians."

"Familiar with the Fengaul are you?" she arced an eyebrow.

"I've found they're fantastic lovers, though their horns do tend to get in the way in certain situations."

"You've glimpsed my scars and know what they mean." She glanced down at the markings on her bare arms. "But how do you know I'm a Leech-doctor and not another type of Runescrawler?"

"Your elegant snuff box." He nodded to the silver box strapped to her belt. "You Leechers enjoy Deathruning people into nothing but dust, which you scoop into your little boxes to snort. Rather perverse if you ask me."

"I suppose a Shamadar would know more than most about the world," she drawled, her eyes leaking disgust. "But I thought most were nomadic brutes, willing to kill anything the least bit monstrous for coin. You, look like a pampered dandy, no fierce hunter. Our soldiers snuck up on you whilst you slept and captured you with ease. Drunk too, apparently."

"Indeed, I'm a disgrace to my Order."

Ranasta's expression remained impassive. Her serenity was at odds compared to most barbarians he'd known, and Fengaul women were usually fiercer than the men.

"What lovely horns you have." He tried again, flashing her his signature grin.

"You aren't a Shamadar of any note." She ignored his words, studying him like a too-lean sow on market day. "How long ago were you made?"

"Only a decade ago." He shrugged, affecting boredom. Smirking like an idiot wouldn't work on her. "I haven't had time to become the type of legendary Shamadar that has innkeeper's tongues wagging and bards singing of my exploits."

"And you never will," she said softly. "Such a shame. I hear only one in fifty survive ingesting the Shamharn ash.

Are the rumours it turns you into monsters on a full moon true?"

"Would you like to wait a few days and find out?" He met her gaze without flinching.

She sighed, plucking a spherical device from her belt. It looked like a large acorn carved out red and green metal, yet Varity's mouth went dry. Sidhe steel, one of the two worst materials to make weapons and armour from, along with Wraithblades.

A child with no training would be deadly with sidhe steeel, let alone the powerful mage before him.

"Ah, I see you know what this is." Her fleshy lips pulled up as she held the seed inches from his face.

Varity could only watch as the tip of the seed birthed a wickedly sharp point, growing gradually. The very base of the seed turned into a pommel as the other half tapered into an exquisite dagger. The blade itself looked wrought out of scarlet and emerald ice, not silver or iron at all. In truth, no one knew what substance the Karna-fae weapons were, only that no armour was safe from them.

"I think I'll keep it like this for now." Ranasta pulled the blade from where it had stopped growing, an inch from his nose. "Perhaps I'll urge it to its full size when I at last hack off your head, yes?"

Varity forced another smile. "It's a pretty little thing, suits you."

Her lips skinned back, revealing too-sharp teeth. He wondered if she'd partaken in cannibalism, like certain Fengaul clans were said to do. Varity promptly stopped himself wondering such dire things once again.

"Okay—" He no longer needed to fake his fear. "I'll tell you what I know about the uprising."

"Revolt, insurrection, not an uprising. These Cimhurans are more barbaric than my people," she snarled. "It's said they drink the blood of scorpions and lay with the red-hide orcs. They've made cities on the backs of long dead Elder Beasts, making homes of bones."

"Well, that's not exclusive to Cimhurans," Varity pointed out.

"We have five hundred soldiers here at Fort Dusthold and occupy six other fortresses around this blighted desert. We'll pick these rebels off, piece by piece, chew them red and spit out their corpses. I'd say we'd raze Cimhura to the ground if it wasn't already a scorched wasteland. You chose incorrectly in aiding these sand worms. Now, you will tell me who hired you and where we can find them."

She gently pressed the tip of her enchanted dagger into the flesh of his arm. "One rune from me will melt your body, disintegrate it into only your dust-essence. I think I'll apply a strength rune, and thus steal all of your strength when I snort your essence."

"True, I'd make a fine transplant. But Death-runing me won't give you the answers you seek," he said carefully, seeing in her eyes she was eager to do it.

Many Leech-Doctors grew addicted to ingesting the essence of their victims, of stealing their attributes to bolster their own. He got the impression this Ranasta was deep in the throes of such addiction. Whatever he told her, she was going to Deathrune him in the end.

"No, I'll merely skill snatch,' she purred, tracing his flesh now, her knife a millimetre from gouging him open. "What shall I steal from you first? A Shamadar without the ability to wield a sword is a terrible thing?"

Heljor! He cursed himself for a fool. The Leech-Doctor didn't have to kill him to take his attribute, she could merely wound him and rip a skill away instead.

"You doubt me?" Ranasta gestured to the litany of runes scarring her arms, many from previous Skill-Snatches. She pointed to one glyph adorning her elbow. "This one was from a University Scholar. He spoke perfect Rynhelm, so I took that from him. This rune I gleaned from a criminal who was exceptionally skilled in archery, I always wanted to learn, but never had the time."

"So, what's the difference between you and other criminals who steal?" Varity asked.

"I do it with the permission of the Dominga," Ranasta replied without missing a beat. "Besides, Skill-Snatching isn't immoral. I can see why Death-runing a person is considered cruel, but merely taking a way a talent they've learned is harmless. They can always relearn it, can't they? Well-" She grinned wickedly. "Not all the time. What if I snatched your ability to breathe, to increase my own; excellent for breathing underwater. Why, you'd slowly suffocate, wouldn't you?"

She moved suddenly, seizing his shirt and ripping it open. Several buttons bounced off the ground like hailstones.

The point of her knife kissed his pectoral muscle as she considered. "It's hard to know what skill you'd least like to lose, without seeing you fight. You were armed with three weapons if I remember. A knife in your boot, a Ghunlin needleshooter, and a griffin-brand-blade. Quite the rare sword I hear. Odds are, you're an exceptionally talented swordsman, or at least think you are. I believe I'll rid you of that ability."

Skerit. He tried not to curse aloud. He should've taken longer to plan out this job. A Leech-Doctor had never figured into his plans. Once she'd runed him, picking up a sword would be like doing so for the very first time. Ranasta was right. This method was far better way of getting him to talk. Problem was, he didn't actually have any information for them. He couldn't give a skerit about their damn war.

"Yes, this will do nicely. Now, if I can just remember the correct rune for swordplay." Ranasta gave her dagger a flourish before pressing it against his chest, without giving him a chance to stall more. No, she was going to take his sword skill away from him first, *then* give him a chance to talk, before ripping away another skill. She might well take his ability to walk away from him, or all the memories he possessed.

He was close to panicking now. All his careful planning decimated. He'd allowed himself to be captured when he knew Fort Dusthold was undermanned, having sent half their force to raid a Cimhuran town just yesterday. Varity thought they would've sent their best warriors with them, not kept a damn Leech-Doctor behind.

A second after the tip of her knife drove into his chest with a scorching sting, a sonorous horn boomed through the castle.

Finally. Varity could almost weep from relief.

Ranasta froze, head jerking to the Ghunlin guard, whose compound eyes met hers in equal confusion. The horn came again, two pulls signalling they were under attack.

"By the Carver," she hissed, hastily moving away. "Fellor, stay with him, we'll see what's going on."

Varity softly exhaled as Ranasta and the hulking Ghunlin left the room.

Fellor looked shaken himself as the horn's last cry echoed faintly off the walls, yet a leering grimace soon replaced it.

"Looks like it's just you an me now, Shamadar."

He ran a hand through his greasy hair, striding back to his tray of tools.

"I was upset Ranasta took you away from me. I was so looking forward to using my girl."

Fellor slowly lifted up the silver bowl taking up most of the tray, revealing the creature within.

Varity expected some venomous insect, not what looked like a miniature tyrannosaur. Varity had seen a fully grown behemoth once, and didn't cherish the thought of encountering one again, yet this reptilian thing would've fit in his hand.

"What is it?" he asked despite himself, though his amusement at the curiosity rather than fear enraged Fellor further.

"A newer species recently discovered in the pirate isles," the Mereshi snapped. "What matters to you is that this tiny thing still has teeth sharp enough to rend flesh."

Fellor's hand shot out to seize the creature by its neck before it scurried away. The animal's squeaking growl was adorable, but the flash of its teeth, like small nails, was not so cute.

"This one I call Daffney." Fellor gave the creature a shake to stop its snapping jaws. "I've been using them to gnaw the stomachs of my patients. Do you know, once I place Daffney and the bowl over you, she'll begin eating into you in her panic to escape. Marvellous, isn't it?"

"It's pretty cruel on Daffney actually."

Fellor's smile sloughed off, his protruding, fish-like eyes darkening.

"That's enough fun and games now, Shamadar. I don't care what information you have, it's time for me to have my own fun."

"You're right." Varity nodded. "You know, your soldier friends may have taken a bag of my jewels, and even tore my earrings out, but they didn't look everywhere on my person."

Varity pressed his tongue against the chip of onyx he'd embedded into his back tooth just this morning. He suffused the jewel with his will, harnessing the onyx's power over stone. At once, the jagged crack in the wall above them widened.

"What are y-" Fellor dropped Daffney back onto the tray, looking up as grains of stone dripped from the ceiling.

Fellor realised too late what Varity was doing. He tried to run, but a boulder-seized chunk of stone fell from the ceiling first, smashing into his skull with all the force Varity could muster.

The Mereshi slammed to the ground face-first, landing at Varity's feet, the chunk of stone rolling away. The rock had dented the top of Fellor's cranium, crushing bone enough that a smidgeon of brain glinted through. Fellor's eyes were open, but he was certainly no longer of the living.

Quickly, Varity struggled with his boots. The chip of onyx was so small it had burned away to nothing with his use of it, leaving him powerless once more. Fellor still had the bag of jewels attached to his belt, but Varity couldn't use the jewels without part of his body being in contact.

With a lot of scuffing and fidgeting, he used one worn boot to wriggle off the other, then stretched out as far as the chair would let him, straining against his chains. After an agonising minute, his big toe snagged the small cloth bag and tugged it free from the corpse's belt.

Varity's heart slammed into his chest. At any moment, Ranasta and the Ghunlin champion could come back and his entire plan would be ruined.

He awkwardly shook the bag upside down, holding its bottom with his toes. The small clump of jewels spilled to the floor, glistening wetly in the ethereal green light of the room.

At last, he pressed a toe against the jewel he needed, moonstone. At his touch and his mind's command, the moonstone ignited with a soft glow and the heavy chains binding him to the chair started to unravel. Like a great snake, the chains curled away before dropping to the stones with a clink.

Varity tensed before snapping the manacles by himself, like he could've done so many hours ago when they were first put on. He could've used moonstone for that too, but he needed to save the few jewels he had left. If the outpost had any other mages like Ranasta, he'd need sorcery to defend himself.

He scooped the stones back into his sack, each of the crystal pieces were jagged, uncut lumps. Only two small pieces of moonstone, one piece of carnelian and three amethysts. He'd purposely hidden his last piece of onyx before he engineered his capture by the soldiers, so they wouldn't safeguard against him using it.

A tiny scraping alerted him to poor Daffney, trying and failing to scramble out of the bowl she'd been deposited in.

"Here you go, lovely." Varity gently but gingerly picked her up, careful of her teeth, before setting her down on the floor, near a wall with cracks enough for her to crawl through. "Be free."

The scaly thing, which would've been a tyrannosaur if it wasn't the size of a mouse, seemed to hiss contentedly before it scarpered towards the wall, slipping in to one of its cracks and going off to be the bane of real mice everywhere.

Shouts of alarm and the stampede of countless pairs of feet started up in the castle high above him. The outpost would be distracted by the battle for some time now. Varity just hoped the creatures he'd lured here would keep the soldiers distracted long enough.

Reminded of just what he'd slathered his shirt and neck with, Varity seized Fellor's waterskin and poured it over himself, hoping it would wash away the rancid, transparent blood he'd used to lure the Scorprarn here.

Varity checked Fellor's body for a weapon, but the corpse held only a small bag of Nystalgia. He tossed the narcotic aside, casting around for something he could use against any guards who stopped him reaching his next destination.

His eyes alighted on the tray of torturing implements. A long, thin scalpel might be his best shot, though he'd have preferred something more substantial. He took a single step forward when he heard heavy steps just outside the chamber.

He instinctively darted to the door's side a second before it swung open.

The Ghunlin Champion stalked in, clicking his mandibles in broken Thaynish. "Fellor, we…" He broke off at the sight of Fellor's broken body.

Varity kicked out from behind, his boot crunching into the Ghunlin's leg behind the knee. As his leg buckled, the Ghunlin reached around with surprising swiftness, his hand smashing into Varity's chest and hurling him into the wall. His teeth chattered and the world blinked as his head hit rock, but he managed to stay on his feet, his vision clearing enough to see the Ghunlin wrench the war hammer off of his back and charge.

Varity made an incoherent sound halfway between a yelp and a curse, rolling beneath the Ghunlin's strike and into the centre of the chamber. The war hammer crashed into the stone where Varity stood seconds before, gouging several chunks out of the wall and almost causing a cave-in.

A low, eerie drone emitted from the Ghunlin Champion as he moved to block the doorway, easily doing so with his ten-foot bulk. With a sword, even a dagger, Varity would fancy his chances, but unarmed--he might as well have been in the Obsidian Ocean without a paddle.

The jewels were his only hope, but the Ghunlin rushed him even as he fumbled with the bag. Varity sidestepped the brute, meaning to use a moonstone to seize the chains once more, but this time use them to strangle the soldier.

Just as his fingers delved into the bag, the Ghunlin feinted another hammer swing, before kicking him instead.

The wind rushed out of him as he was flung through the air to land back in the torture chair, his sack of jewels flying out of his hand. Varity writhed on the iron chair, trying to gasp oxygen back into his lungs as the Ghunlin raised his war hammer high.

Varity waited until the very last second, the war hammer already hurtling down, before springing from the chair and seizing the scalpel from the tool tray. He leaped up, plunging the point of the scalpel into one of the Ghunlin's compound eyes. The insectoid membrane exploded in a welter of gelatinous fluid and the Ghunlin's droning contorted into a screech.

The soldier dropped his hammer, pressing a hand to his punctured eye, mandibles quivering wildly. His other hand shot out to snatch Varity's throat.

He tried in vain to break the Ghunlin's grip, but they both toppled to the ground, his enemy atop him, using enough strength to crush his windpipe. Shamadar healed quickly, but they could die as well as anyone if you shoved a sword into their hearts or brains. Varity reckoned he wouldn't heal from having his head popped right off either, which the Ghunlin was near about doing.

His vision blackened at the edges, his opponent's eye juice leaking onto his face.

He was suffocating, the world starting to swim. Frantically, he seized a mandible in each hand and wrenched with all his might. The Ghunlin screeched for a second, before Varity ripped the mandibles from his face in a fresh wave of crimson.

The Ghunlin Champion rolled off of him, spasming violently. Varity scrambled to his feet and put an end to the soldier's suffering, crushing his head to pulp with his own war hammer.

He stumbled back into the chair--gasping. His throat was on fire, and the Ghunlin's kick might've ruptured his spleen. His larynx certainly felt crushed, but as he sat slumped, he felt his body begin its healing. He didn't have time to spare, however, and forced himself back to his feet.

Hastily, Varity retrieved his jewels and fled the torture chamber, taking the war hammer with him.

He emerged into a dark stone passage, splashed liberally with hard-packed dirt and smudged with soot. The only flickering light came from a sputtering sconce high on the wall.

As he expected, he'd been thrown into a room at the lowest levels of the castle. In fact, he was sure he was in the dungeons now. His only route was left, so he started down it, ears pricked for anyone approaching. He heard only the faint sounds of battle, muffled by the several floors of ancient stone rising above.

The passage felt more like a tunnel, the yellow-brown stone was infested with tendrils of what resembled ivy, yet the crawling vines were spiked, like cacti.

He began to pass holes set in the wall, festooned with rusted metal bars, cells. The first few cells were empty, but by the scent of sweat and urine, others were occupied.

He shuffled further down the corridor, peering into the next cell along.

A short shape huddled in the shadows, yet stirred at his approach. A little dwarf girl looked up at him, practically still a child. Most dwarves he'd encountered were men, tough as old shoe leather, with grander beards than he could ever grow and usually with a love for sailing, but nearly all of them enslaved.

The prisoner before him didn't have the tattoos across her chin and cheeks like most female dwarves, but she did bear a slave brand on her forearm.

"Is today to be my execution?" She croaked.

She seemed to be under the impression he'd come to lead her to the gallows, perhaps that was what all the prisoners rotting in these dungeons awaited, that and regular torture sessions with Varity's recently deceased friend.

"Please, did the guards tell Lord Duvain I'm sorry? They promised they would." The dwarf inched closer to the bars of her cell.

Tear tracks trailing down her cheeks were the only passingly clean patches amidst the filth covering her face. Even the two small horns either side of her head were covered in grime. "Please, tell the lord, Mevrin won't ever take an extra loaf of bread again. Tell him she's the perfect slave. Duvain won't really behead me, will he?"

"Sorry, no time for chatting. How about freedom instead?"

The dwarf stumbled away from him, confusion warring with hatred on her face. "Is this come cruel jest? One of the other soldiers pretended to release me."

"No time for jests neither. Got time to help you though." He didn't really. Every minute was precious. He should be saving his moonstone too. If he burned it all away before his mission was done, engineering his own capture would've been for naught.

Varity knew he couldn't leave the prisoners here though, especially the girl now he'd seen her.

He pulled the moonstone from his bag, which glowed with an ethereal light as he suffused it with his will. Directing his thoughts toward the cell's lock enabled him to snap it in half with ease.

Mevrin pushed the door open slowly, gaze darting back to him repeatedly, as if expecting he'd shove her back in and slam the door in her face.

The next cell along contained two prisoners. One was a Cimhuran man, his long black hair twined with scarlet locks and shaved bald on the left side of his skull, like the majority of his people. He wore only a threadbare pair of breeches, his bare torso covered in pale red tattoos, another Cimhuran custom.

His jail mate was a Rynhelm. Like all of his race, he was tall, muscled and humanoid, save for being covered in black fur and having the head of a goat. He looked frightening there in the dark, his horizontal pupils trained on Varity. Yet most Rynhelm were prone to peace, unless provoked.

"It's your lucky day, boys." Varity suffused his moonstone again to set them free.

The two prisoners edged out of the cell with the same uncertainty Mevrin had possessed.

"You aren't from the Dragonshade tribe, are you?" he asked the Cimhuran, just in case.

He frowned. "I'm one of the Goldnails, my tribe is far from here."

"Then I hope you find them again. Here take this. I prefer swords myself." He tossed him the war hammer before turning to the last cell, containing an Asgan ape-man.

"May the Carver garnish you with glory, friend," the fellow, more gorilla than man, bowed to Varity as his cell was unlocked. The Asgan spoke perfect Thaynish, even with a refined accent.

"Don't worry about it. Though if any of you are bards, feel free to sing about the saintly Varity Varen, who liberated you this day. Run along now and make merry."

Four prisoners running loose should provide further distractions he could use, though Varity did hope they made it out alive.

He stiffened as a hand reached out to him from behind, before he realised it was Mevrin and she meant him no harm. Her hand lingered on his arm for a second as she nodded through tear-filled eyes. He wasn't used to anyone trying to touch him without a weapon or sorcery in their hands.

"Thank you, stranger," Mevrin murmured. "I'll never forget this."

The other prisoners had already fled ahead with barely a thanks, but Varity didn't blame them. Freedom after so long must seem a trick and it was something that could still be ripped cruelly away until they'd put many miles between them and Fort Dusthold, if they managed to get out undetected.

Varity just nodded awkwardly at the dwarf, unsure how to react to her gratitude. "You're small, try and find a side door and don't stop running until this castle is a dot on the horizon."

"I will." She smiled at him with genuine warmth, another image he hadn't seen in a long time, before jogging away down the dark passage, leaving him alone once more.

Varity leaned back and gave the prisoners a head-start before marching on. The soldiers might almost be done fighting the Scorprarn now. He had to reach the West tower quickly.

As the shadowed passage sloped upwards, a duo of surprised shouts were swiftly stifled. By the time Varity reached the corridor's end, the two soldiers on gaoler duty still sat at their card game, but they'd never finish it.

The barred gate out of the dungeons screamed on its hinges as he pushed it open, emerging into the castle proper. Here, the Dominga had at least attempted to recreate the garish decadence they liked to splash about everywhere they conquered.

Carpets from Kufrin and Rynhelm crafted pottery filled the corridors, and exquisite tapestries lined the walls, which were decidedly cleaner. The spiked ivy couldn't be banished it seemed, but at least the dark yellow of the huge bricks had been polished. Varity imagined Fort Dusthold had been a castle belonging to native Cimhurans some years past, renamed recently.

The sounds of battle were louder now, and he saw no one else as he climbed several flights of steps. At last, he encountered a window and promptly stuck his head out, surveying what his machinations had wrought.

Perhaps as much as four hours ago, before the sun had truly risen and the patter of a mild meteor storm still raged, Varity had snuck as close to Dusthold as he'd dared and planted the Foulworm corpse, hidden strategically between two boulders, metres from Dusthold's outer wall. The ten-foot-long Foulworms were named for the rancid stench they oozed, an aroma that grew even greater in death. It might've stank worse than an orcish privy to most, but the scent was irresistible to Scorprarn, and they could detect it from miles away. Varity had also rubbed his own shirt and neck with Foulworm blood for good measure, before camping in the abandoned town ruins close to Dusthold, where the soldier patrol could easily capture him.

Once they found Foulworm, digesting their favourite prey would only made Scorprarn hunger for more. Conveniently there was a castle chock-full of more prey, and Varity's own Foulworm scent would also draw the monsters in. The Scorprarn might still make a beeline for him now, since the water he'd doused on himself probably hadn't washed away all the Foulworm's stink.

The window he leaned from hung above the castle courtyard, showing a scene of brutal chaos below. Dominga soldiers, men and women of races high and midling, scurried around like headless chickens. Only a skeleton crew manned the fort, but the Dominga had been smart enough to leave dozens to hold against attack.

The Scorprarn scaled the outer wall, climbing up with their hooked pincers and vaulting onto the parapets, hissing and screeching. The Cimhurans claimed you could scarcely throw a stone without hitting a hidden Scorprarn. It looked like they'd been right with how many of the monsters had been lured by his bait. Many had spilled over the battlements and into the courtyard beyond. Still, this was a Dominga outpost and they'd defeat the surprise intruders before long. But all Varity needed was a distraction.

His stomach dropped as he noticed a flying figure amongst the soldiers. *Skerit, they have a Jewelburner here too!*

The mage flew up from the courtyard and onto the battlements, a glowing agate in his hand.

There were a lot more jewels that could suffused for their sorcery than the few Varity was attuned to. This other Jewelburner could obviously utilise the element of air with his agate. *Oh, and he can suffuse rubies too.* He watched the mage fling his other arm out, scarlet light wreathing his fist before the glow contorted into a torrent of fire that reduced one Scorprarn monster to ash.

He already had to watch out for Ranasta, Varity likely couldn't take on two mages at once. Many companions told Varity he was arrogant, and they had a point, but he wasn't deluded.

He leaned further out of the window, scouring around for something he could do to improve his chances. To his joy, he spied a metal ballista atop the eastern tower, roughly two hundred yards above him. The ballista was already loaded with a bolt a metre long. Varity would rather take out his rival Jewelburner by surprise then face him in the open, where more soldiers would doubtless be drawn by the battle. He pulled the moonstone from his bag, clenching it tightly in his fist as it ignited with a ghostly glow.

The mage leaped around on the battlements, using his agate now to shove a Scorprarn back with a buffet of wind.

Varity felt sweat bead on his brow as he took possession of the ballista with his moonstone's control over metal. The giant crossbow slowly moved into position, as if directed by a phantom, as Varity aimed just right.

The Jewelburner flew high into the air again, above the battlements to survey the other Scorprarn attempting to climb up below.

Now!

The bolt exploded out of the ballista a moment after Varity envisioned it, feeling tiny grains of the moonstone burn away in his hand. The mage had his back to the ballista, and suspected nothing until the metre-long bolt flew into his back and lodged halfway through his chest on the other side. The Jewelburner dropped like a tomato, liquid of the same hue leaking out of him.

"Tough way to go," Varity murmured. "Should've served better masters."

He ducked back inside the window as confused cries rang out below. Perhaps some soldiers would be stupid enough to believe the ballista fired of its own volition, a faulty trigger. Yet Varity knew better. Despite the attack on the fort, his disappearance from the torture chamber might've been noticed by now. The alarm for his recapture might've already gone up, just lost amongst the chaos. He swiftly ran from the window and up to the next floor, before soldiers swarmed to his location.

He was in the middle of a wide corridor when he heard hurried footsteps pounding his way, yet with no doorway to duck into, he instead grabbed for the pouch at his belt, fishing out a carnelian just in time.

Half a dozen guards rounded the corridor, the woman at their head almost running straight into him.

She stopped, the look of shock on her face mirroring his own.

The men were all Household guard, following Lady Esmer of House Rothtis to the fight.

Varity didn't really know her, in truth, yet he'd never expected to encounter anyone with even a passing familiarity so far from home, and of the life he'd lived before becoming a Shamadar.

They'd likely shared a number of feasts and balls together, maybe even danced a ditty or two in the endless swapping of partners at one of the festivals. House Rothtis was a noble family of Galbadir, just like Varity's former House Varen. Of course, he'd long been exiled and stripped of his own title as Lord, and his father vowed to execute him on the spot if he ever saw Varity again. He would've been worm-food already if it wasn't for the Shamadar Legion recruiting him on death row.

Unfortunately, Lady Esmer and her armoured guards already had weapons drawn, and they wasted no time pointing right at him.

"Who are you?" Lady Esmer demanded. "And what in heljor are you doing here?"

She surveyed his dusty breeches and damp, only half buttoned-up shirt. "I'm…the Lady Tivrin's personal, uh…strumpet."

He subtly suffused his shard of carnelian in the hand he kept down at his side.

"House Tivrin isn't even stationed at this outpost, I-" Esmer's eyes widened as she noticed the black rings around his irises. "You're him, the Shamadar they captured? Guards!"

"No, really," he said, backing away as Esmer's guards encircled him, their steel ready to skewer. "I'm no Shamadar."

Pale trails of violet light leaked from his carnelian, wafting in the air, barely visible, swimming about Lady Esmer and her guards' heads.

"You…you're not?" Esmer's brows knitted into a frown as she studied him. "Do I know you…I feel we've met before."

The carnelian sizzled in his hand as he desperately poured his will into it. He'd suffused the jewel countless times, but making seven people at once believe every word you say was a struggle.

"No, my lady. I am but a humble harlot. The Lady Tivrin arrived here two days ago. Now, you really must be off to help the soldiers battle those pesky Scorprarn."

"Yes, I…of course. Come, men." Lady Esmer nodded before raising her katana and running past him, leading her guards away.

Varity breathed a sigh of relief, slipping the carnelian, which had burned away to a third of the size, back into his bag.

He'd be feeling the side effects of suffusing carnelian soon, and the side effects of moonstone were already hitting him.

Varity's skill at Jewelburning was good enough that the side effects only troubled him when he suffused a lot. Firing the ballista was enough to make him lightheaded and dizzy now. He stumbled down the corridor, trying to ignore that the walls kept seeming to slip away from him as the world whirled. The side effects should wear off shortly, but he didn't have time to sit and wait.

As far as Jewelburners went, he wasn't among the best. He'd encountered other mages whose mastery over their jewels put him to shame.

He wanted to sprint through the castle, but the dizziness made him settle on a brisk walk, which saw him almost walk straight into the wall a couple of times. He searched for a route that would take him to the West Tower. That was where he'd smelled brimstone when the guards first brought him in. That's where the Dominga would be keeping her.

As his boots echoed off the stone, he spied a decorative onyx bowl on a windowsill. The bowl was small, perhaps an ash tray for the cigarillos wealthy merchants and nobles often smoked. Worth a pretty penny, and better yet, the onyx it was hewn out of could be suffused. Varity snatched up the bowl and dropped it into his pocket, adding petty theft to his list of crimes against the Dominga.

The castle corridors remained deserted, as the clash of steel and shouts of desperate men continued to cry out.

At last, the dizziness abated, and Varity started to pick up the pace. Judging by his glimpses through arrow slits, he was nearing the fort's outer wall now. He'd have to go out where the fighting was thickest, but he should be able to reach the West tower far quicker that way. He reached the castle's top floor and as he wheeled around a corner, he nearly knocked a woman on her rump.

"What in Carver's name!" she squawked.

He almost thought Dusthold castle was haunted with how dreadfully pale she was, though her parchment-thin flesh was far too wrinkled to be corporeal. The old crone was only half his height, and a nun by her red and gold livery and headdress.

"You, boy, what are you doing?"

"Narthin mooch," he spluttered, unable to articulate properly, the side effects of suffusing carnelian taking hold of him.

The nun looked up at him with a stunned sneer, one gnarled old hand resting on her sword hilt.

Even the holy men and women devoted to serving the Carver wore swords, and most knew a little of how to use them. He looked down at the nun, feeling a little ashamed of what he was about to do, but needs must.

"I require your seword."

"What are you blathering about?"

"Yorr swerd." He gestured to her basket-hilted cutlass.

The nun's beady eyes widened as she took him in. "You! I know your vile, demonic kind. You will burn in heljor. Blasphemer. I shall sentence you to hang myself, and let the crows feast on your entrails."

"Bit harshsss."

Unfortunately, his carnelian wouldn't work again so soon. Varity sighed, stepping closer and cracking the nun in the head with a light chop. She wilted with a moan, unconscious. He should've killed her, in case she awoke before he was done here, but even Varity couldn't bring himself to murder a nun in cold blood.

He took her sword, before hefting up her body and slinging it across his shoulders. He needed to get her out of view, partly so she didn't get accidentally trampled by anyone, but also to cover his own tracks. He kicked open a nearby door, depositing the woman of the cloth in a cramped privy. "Sorry old girl. Try not to be so eager to execute people next time."

He darted back into the passage and down another, using the windows to navigate his position. In only moments he reached a door leading directly onto the battlements. Battle raged right outside, but he couldn't see another way to the westmost tower. It was his only chance, and the soldiers would wipe out the Scorprarn soon.

After a deep breath, Varity seized the heavy iron door and hauled it open, emerging into the anarchy of combat. The oppressive air of the humid castle evaporated. For once, a pleasant breeze soared through Cimhura and washed over him. The relief lasted only a second, before the stench of blood and bile, sweat and fear, splashed over him.

It wasn't a war before him, not a great battle either, but a plethora of individual struggles. All the way down the battlements, two to three soldiers clustered a Scorprarn each.

Scarlet splotches streaked stone, but pools of black fluid were more prominent. Only six Scorprarn remained here, and a handful more still waged havoc in the courtyard below.

He chanced a look over the parapet, seeing no more Scorprarn scrabbling up the walls nor lurking in the desert below. The last of them were being picked off now. He might only have minutes to finish his mission.

Varity sprinted down the battlements, with room just enough to skirt the first trio of guards who didn't notice him, busy as they were with the five-foot-tall arachnid.

The duo of guards ahead however, just finished hacking their opponent to ruin when Varity approached.

Both soldiers wore identical expressions of astonishment and before Varity could try to claim he was a Dominga soldier too, just without his armour, the hasty bastards went for him.

"The escaped Shamadar," one bellowed at the top of his lungs, just what Varity needed. He decided to shut that one up first.

Both men advanced towards him, but Varity slid through them like water, flicking his sword out seemingly careless as he went. His casual strike slashed into the pit of one guard's knee, severing the tendon and causing him to flail to the ground.

The mouthy guard opened his maw to shout about Varity again, even as he swung at his head. Varity ducked the blow, before stepping smoothly beneath his opponent's guard and driving his blade up through the man's chin. His attempted shout turned to a squawk as Varity let him fall, before promptly booting the other man off the battlements and into the courtyard below.

He resumed racing across the wall, four more guards fought a particularly enraged Scorprarn ahead. The fight was so frenetic, there wasn't room enough to run around them. Instead, Varity sprung onto the nearest crenulation and launched himself inhumanly high, landing on the other side of the commotion.

Three soldiers stood in his path now, two dusk elves with skin of lightest blue, and an orc with grey hide and dirt encrusted tusks. The trio weren't only ready for Varity, but they called down to the milling soldiers below for aid. Fortunately for him, one Scorprarn was blocking the steps from the courtyard to the battlements, though the rush of men would soon do away with him.

Knowing time was fast running out, Varity ripped the moonstone back out of his pouch, suffusing it desperately. The moonstone ignited with a lurid light, a moment before he directed its sorcery to seize the iron his enemies wore. With a huge surge of sorcery, Varity flung his arm sharply to the left. The soldier's armour crumpled as they were flung hard to the left, the two dusk elves toppled over the wall like bouncing stones, whilst the orc dropped his blade to seize hold of a crenulation and prevent his perilous fall. The soldier delayed his flight at least, as Varity seized the orc's fallen sword with sorcery, levitating it into the air before throwing it into the orc's chest a moment after he'd dragged himself back onto the wall. The soldier spun in a half circle before joining his brethren in their trip to the desert sixty metres below.

The single surge of power burned away near half of his moonstone, but Varity cared little. The odour of brimstone was starting to quench all other smells. The West tower was only metres away.

He rolled between the next group of battling guards, with an agility and skill he wished some of his Shamadar companions were here to see. He'd no time to congratulate himself though. The last Scorprarn had bested the soldier trying to drive him off the top of the castle, instead making a smear out of the man's skull.

Well, I suppose I brought this on myself. Varity rushed to meet the abomination.

He reared back, once, twice, thrice, narrowly avoiding his head getting lopped off by abnormally large pincers.

The Scorprarn stood only a head shorter than a man, its body covered in pale orange chitin. The arachnid monster looked most like a scorpion, complete with a stinger swaying at its back with a mind of its own. Aside from a gaping maw, the thing's face was indistinguishable at the top of its vaguely human torso, but it did possess to eyes on stalks that wriggled up where a head might be. With its thick, human-like legs and muscled body, Varity reckoned the Scorprarn more resembled some demented form of lobster and man than a giant scorpion. Still, it was the pincers you needed to watch out far, sharp as any sword. Both pincers hurtled toward Varity now, click-clacking through the air.

He danced back, parrying with his blade. The pincers scrapped off of his steel, unaffected. Scorprarn were hard to kill, their pincers tough as stone and their chitin like suits of armour, but it was Varity's job to know how to kill the many monsters of the world.

He ducked a third pincer blow that swept for his head, then slashed up as he rose, hacking both of the Scorprarn's eye stalks in half like flower stems. With a spurt of black ichor, the thing fell squealing. As the Scorprarn writhed, Varity sank his blade deep into the soft patch of flesh by the armpit, the only place the chitin didn't cover. The monster went still as Varity pierced its heart.

He wrenched his cutlass back out with a squelch and hurried the rest of the way across the parapet, at last reaching his destination.

The steel door to the West tower was doubly reinforced and bolted, with a padlock the size of his head securing it. Varity pressed his moonstone against the door, using its power to swiftly unlock the several bolts at the top of the door, before splitting the padlock in two. Even with his Shamadar given strength, it was an effort to drag the door open and slip inside.

The heat hit him at once, like he'd stepped inside the furnace of a blacksmith's forge.

There were no sconces on the walls, or hanging gaslight globes at all, yet an otherworldly light far below allowed him to make out the circular tower around him, and the spiralling steps ringing the wall. He started down the curling path, thinking how moronic the builders had been seeing as there was no rail to stop one from slipping and plummeting to probable death. The fall wouldn't be fatal for Varity, being a Shamadar, though the chance he might fall into a waiting dragons' mouth did make things more perilous.

Halfway down the dark tower, the beast's tremendous form began to take shape and by now its laboured breath filled his keen ears. If this tower was blistering as a smithy, the monster's breath was like a bellows. He could only discern a much more solid shadow amongst the others, but she stirred at his approach.

Varity slowed a few steps from the bottom of the tower. The scrape of claws on stone would've made him stop entirely, but the rustle of chains told him the monster was trapped. For now.

He was grateful that at least the tower was lit by two sconces on the its ground floor, until he realised the two orbs of red light were the dragon's eyes. Boiling hatred and wrath poured out of the crimson caverns set in that basilisk-like head.

He did freeze in place now, letting his eyes adjust and praying he wasn't a second from being eaten.

Slowly, the scene before him came into focus. She was as lethal and beautiful as he'd been told. A Panthera Draconai, named for its black mane of wiry long hairs around the neck. Panthera Draconai were one of the smallest dragon types, yet she was still the size of a mammoth, and that was before you added the wing span.

Perhaps Varity was imagining things, but the hate and fury seemed to leak away from those eyes as they pierced his own, as if she recognised, he wasn't one of those come here to hurt her.

Several iron rings, the size of wagon wheels, had chains wrapped securely around them, their ends constricting each of the dragon's huge legs. A giant metal device had been fitted around the dragon's snout, another chain on each side helping to pin the poor beast to the ground. He suspected the iron muzzle prevented the creature from opening its maw and unleashing her fire. Worst of all, both of her wings were pinned to the stone, driven through at ends by iron spikes.

Many of her scales had already been pulled away, some partially scabbed over by weeping crust, others glistened with red raw skin beneath. The soldiers here had already started dismantling her for parts.

Foolish, or deranged, hunters were always trying to nab a dragon. One could get rich off of selling their scales for materials, or their glands to make narcotics out of. But Varity could guess what the soldiers here intended for this specimen. Once they'd taken all the resources from her, he was almost certain Ranasta would Deathrune the poor thing. Taking transplants from beasts was far more dangerous for a Leech-doctor, yet he'd heard of it being done. There were stories some mages had managed to take a dragon's fire breathing ability through Deathruning.

This Ranasta woman had to be suicidal, or else insanely devoted to the Dominga. All the reports of Leech-doctors snorting dragon transplants ended with them dying after the transplant's magic wore off, their bodies expiring as their bodies burned from the inside out. All Leech-doctors had only imbibed a dragon's essence to use in battle, but spewing fire down upon the enemy came with the ultimate price. Still, the destruction Ranasta could cause before the transplant destroyed her would be immeasurable.

"You must be Eshindra." That's what the Dragonshade tribe named her, the deity they'd worshiped for generations. Varity wondered if Eshindra recognised her own name.

Eshindra moaned softly as she gazed deep into his eyes, a clear, frightful intelligence in her own. As a Shamadar, battling all manner of monsters was an inevitability, but Varity had never been so close to a dragon before, nor stared one in the eye. He could well believe the legends that some dragons could speak now. He definitely sensed Eshindra's emotions; they came in waves like the sheer heat radiating off of her. All her hatred had long melted away, replaced with agony.

"Easy girl," he whispered, edging off of the steps and closer to her.

He'd known the Dominga would've had her trapped here somehow, but he'd assumed they had a Runescrawler other than Ranasta, or perhaps a Spellsinger, to keep the dragon docile. There were certain songs and runes some mages could utilise to keep even a dragon paralysed, or imprisoned by other means. It seemed the Dominga force at Fort Dusthold were content on just pinning their prize beast to the ground by force.

The chains shouldn't be a problem with his moonstone, but removing the spikes in her wings might well cause her enough pain that she'd kill him the moment he tried.

Well, he didn't have time to formulate a better plan. He was already gambling that no one had seen him slip inside the tower, but he'd definitely been spotted by soldiers in the courtyard below the battlements. Even now, they could be realising where he must've gone.

Hoping that with the muzzle on, he should be okay from errant teeth crunching on his head, Varity swiftly stepped forward and plucked the spear-sized spike from her left wing.

The dragon roared so loud Varity felt his eardrum burst apart. He clapped a hand to his ear even as he leaped away from Eshindra's writhing body. Her tail lashed from side to side frantically.

He winced as he felt his inhuman healing close his eardrum back together.

"Sorry, just one more girl." He circled round her, hurrying a mere foot from her masked head. Those scarlet eyes bore into him like stars, yet the hate hadn't returned. Hopefully, that meant he wouldn't be her first victim once she was free.

He yanked the second spike out and this time she only groaned mournfully, her great body tensing. A speck of her blood splashed onto his hand, hot as boiling water. He cast the second spike aside and ignited his moonstone, using its power to unravel the heavy links of chains wrapped so tight around her legs they'd split the flesh.

The dragon appeared to sigh with relief as the jagged metal fell away. This close, he saw how her claws, each one half a metre long, had gouged deep scrapes into the stone floor, despite the constraints.

The giant, yet sinuous muscles of her legs flexed as she stretched them, yet still shook her head irritably.

"I know, I know." He said soothingly, moving back to her head and the last contraption imprisoning her.

He paused, thinking things through and trying to predict how she'd react. If there was only one thing everyone could agree on with dragons, it was their unpredictability.

Eshindra might go for him straight away, regardless if she was aware he'd freed her. The soldiers had likely starved her and her hunger might be too consuming, despite the fact Panthera Draconai didn't regularly consume humans. Or, she could hurt herself in a desperate attempt to escape the tower the moment she was able. Either way, Varity doubted she'd wait patiently for him to create her escape route. He decided to make it before removing her muzzle, even if it would alert the soldiers and bring them down upon him.

He sheathed his stolen sword, keeping the moonstone in his left hand but pulling out the stolen onyx ashtray with the other. He lifted the onyx high, toward the tower's roof, and ignited the small bowl.

Dust rained down like a miniature waterfall, before the stones cracked and part of the ceiling caved in on itself. The ashtray's rim started to melt, onyx dripping down both sides in runny streaks. Several large chunks of old stone plummeted from the roof and he quickly shot them to the left, to land on the worn steps rather than himself or the dragon. With a huge grinding screech, he dislodged another hole in the roof, and another, until a gaping maw revealed the sky above. The gap wasn't near big enough for the dragon of course, but since his onyx bowl had burned away to the size of a pea, he hoped Eshindra could do the rest.

The chains snapped taut on her muzzle as she gazed at the sky, her wings quivering in anticipation.

"That's it. You've got the idea."

A multitude of shouts and cries of alarm followed the cave-in he'd wrought. The soldiers were coming.

Varity bent down and grabbed the contraption locking the dragon in place. His moonstone had eroded away to the size of a marble now, yet it was enough to unlock the three intertwining latches on the muzzle itself, and then each of the two chains connected to the rings on the ground. When the last chain snapped in half, she was free.

Eshindra shook her great head from side to side, and Varity straightened quickly, preparing to dive away should she open that terrible maw. Instead she nudged him ever so gently with the tip of her snout, her way of a thank you.

"My pleasure. I can see why the Dragonshade tribe say you're sacred."

Voices erupted high above them, followed by the clink of armour and rustle of swords as soldiers ran into the tower.

The dragon turned sharply and Varity edged back as she growled low in her throat.

A dozen men emerged from the gloom, lit by the dragons glow a second before she unleashed.

The liquid torrent of gold engulfed the soldiers, melting their armour to mercury, their flesh to bubbling pink sap and charring their very bones. The few parts of their armour managing not to liquify clattered to the steps.

Varity was forced into a crouch, buffeted by the overwhelming beats of the dragon's wings as she took to the air, slowly revolving as she levitated up, slowly at first, but building in speed.

Eshindra arched her great back and roared once more, this time in defiance and joy. Her flight quickened astonishingly and she erupted through the roof, only her head cleared through the hole he'd made, and the rest of her smashed the surrounding stone apart, shattering outwards.

A chorus of surprised bellows turned to screams of absolute terror before cutting off suddenly as Varity heard the rush of fire drench them. *Play with dragons, you're gonna get burnt.*

He hoped Eshindra had the sense to fly away quickly and not stay to destroy all those who'd kept her in captivity. Varity knew he'd do the latter, but the fort still had at least Ranasta on the premises and maybe more mages. If the dragon was killed or recaptured, his whole mission would've been for naught.

As he raced back up the steps, stepping in puddles that had once been men, he was deafened by the flap of wings which seemed to grow steadily fainter. *Good.* She was as smart as she looked.

Still, there wasn't time to congratulate himself yet. He still had to escape himself. Getting to the stables would be his best shot.

He was two thirds of the way up the tower when a steel shadow emerged above.

"Richard, Edorf. Did the bitch get either of you?" The soldier cried out.

The orc's eyes yellow bulged in shock as Varity spun out of the shadows toward him. The soldier reacted quickly, lunging with his spear.

Varity merely sidestepped the stab and shoved the orc tumbling through the dark to land below with a crunch.

He reached the top of the tower and held his blade ready as he stepped back onto the battlements, slipping out in a crouch. Sunlight pricked his eyes, causing him to blink rapidly. He'd forgotten it was still only noon, the tower's insides had been like eternal night.

The parapet was empty of all guards. He exhaled in relief. The reason, of course, was the anarchy his new dragon friend had wrought. The courtyard below was filled with soldiers. Half of them were melted bodies, flesh forever fused to their armour, whilst the other half milled like hornets in a broken nest. Most hurried with buckets of water sloshing in their hands, throwing what they could on the dozen small fires raging.

Many of the giant slabs across the courtyard were scorched black, and Varity noticed with a fresh wave of queasiness that some of the black, scorched things were skeletons.

Those not hurrying to beat down fires, were the wounded, crying out for relief from their burns. The stench of sizzling skin was nauseating. The chaos was good for one thing, however. No one took notice of Varity where he crouched and he thought it'd be easy to sneak his way to the stables and steal a mount. He was almost at the finish line now.

No sooner had he taken a single step, then a strange rush of wind made him jerk upright. She landed a metre away from him on battlements, the sharp snap of her cloak whipping in the air.

Ranasta glared bloody murder at him, teeth bared as she practically frothed at the mouth. She'd leaped up to the castle parapet all the way from the courtyard, a height of forty feet.

The poisonous yellow of her eyes had all but vanished, suffocated by severely dilated pupils. She must've snorted a lot of transplants, the veins of her face throbbed, ready to burst from the skin.

"What have you done?" she snarled, spit flying.

"What my employer asked." He was impressed with how suave and at ease his voice sounded as he fell into fighting stance.

Her muscles bulged within her leather jerkin, unnaturally thick, three times as large as when he'd first seen her. She'd snorted a powerful strength transplant for sure, maybe more than one. She would've imbibed an agility transplant too, to explain how she'd jumped up to him. Varity wondered idly how many victims Ranasta had murdered, turned to dust she could snort to possess her current power.

"You…" Ranasta faltered, looking ready to pop several blood vessels. "Were you ever a spy for the Cimhurans?"

"Sorry. I've led you on a merry little go-around haven't I?" He laughed at her; he didn't know why. Maybe one final chuckle before death. Varity was confident in his own abilities, but not delusional. He'd felt Ranasta's power in the torture chamber, and it looked like she'd ingested far more transplants than any Leech-Doctor usually partook. Worse, her sidhe-steel sword would've been a problem in the hands of an average thug, let alone a mage who could've stolen the skills from a master swordsman for all he knew.

Ranasta plucked the seed from her belt now, and it grew once again to a dagger in her hands, only this time it kept growing, until a six-foot-tall curved blade of translucent emerald and sapphire glimmered in her grip.

"I'll try not to kill you quick," she ground out between clenched teeth, her every muscle spasming with barely restrained energy. "I shall leave you alive enough to be hung from these walls, your intestines dangling out of you as bait for the crows."

"Well I do pride myself on my generosity, and I do like feeding birds. But what is it with the women in this Fort and their desire to see crows feasting upon me? I-" Varity cut off with a yelp as Ranasta charged him.

She swung her giant wraithblade, bringing it down to cleave his entire body in half. Varity threw himself to the ground just in time. Instead, her sidhe steel crashed into the tower door, shearing through iron like paper. Varity flipped to his feet behind her, but even as he went to strike, she whirled with frightening, inhuman speed.

His sword was still swinging when her blade smashed into it, snapping the cutlass into shards. He swore, staggering back under the blow as the remnants of his weapon fell around him.

Ranasta's cackle was reminiscent of a shrieking cat as she lunged again. Varity leaped to the side, a split-second before her sword slammed down on the crenulation where he'd stood, shattering a turret to pieces. Her swing was indomitable, but left her open. Now unarmed, Varity directed a punch first to her jaw, then to her stomach in rapid succession. Both blows felt like punching a rock wall, his fists damn near breaking.

"Skerit!" He swore, changing his plans to instead run. Before he could attempt it, her own fist snaked out. He whirled wildly away, but wasn't fast enough. Instead of connecting with his jaw and likely ripping it off of his face, her fist grazed his chest. The sheer force of the sorcery-infused blow shoved him violently back, right off the top of the parapet.

Varity was aware he was falling. The world seemed to slip by, and then it was upside down and all the breath rushed out of him. His arm crunched, snapped and splintered. He lay on the courtyard, an agonised groan ripping out of him. Varity knew he should be on his feet. He was no good here. But when he tried, he only managed to roll on his side, mouth wide open as his body continued to seek breath.

Ranasta landed beside him, with such force her boots cracked the stone slab. "You've ruined everything, Shamadar! Do you know how much it took to capture the drake?"

Varity had just managed to crawl to all fours when she kicked him so hard that he twirled in a spiral through the air before landing back on the tiles. Two, perhaps three broken ribs added to his misery. The broken bones would heal far quicker than normal, but such injuries would take him an hour or two, no help now.

Few fires still burned around him and most of the wounded had been carried away or silenced. A chorus of jeering soldiers lined the edges of his vision, swarming around, eager to watch him die. They made a makeshift audience for their duel, ready to fall upon him like a pack of velociraptors in the unlikely event Varity was victorious.

"Actually." Varity wheezed, struggling to his feet. "Drakes are mere cousins to proper dragons, if you must know."

He wrenched last piece of moonstone out of his pocket, sucking in breath. He willed the stone to burn, but Ranasta surged toward him, lightning fast, snatching at his head and gripping tight.

"Not the hair-" He cut off as she swung him by his long locks, wrenching a clump free as he took a second flight. Varity felt more ribs snap as he crashed into a wooden pillar and slid down it, nearly cracking the beam in half.

Vision swimming, breath shuddering, he spotted some sort of construction around him, and that he lay before the castle stables. The splintered wood continued to break, sounding like a dozen gun shots. For one wild moment he thought the giant wooden contraption was going to fall on top of him and he scurried back out from underneath it.

Ranasta swung her sword in a vast arc, slicing yet more of his hair as she came within an inch of cleaving his head off as he dived and rolled.

"You've ruined my barnet, woman." He roared, igniting his moonstone and pulling a sword to him from across the courtyard, wrenching it from the corpse of a soldier with a squelch.

Ranasta flew at him, her sidhe sword moving in her hands like it weighed nothing. Varity reared away from the tempest of her blows, doing his utmost just to stay alive.

At last, he slid beneath one of her slashes and managed to rake his sword across her stomach. The witch might have overdosed on sorcery and wielded an enchanted sword, but she wore no armour. Her scarlet cloak parted like a cobweb as his blow sliced a wide gouge into her stomach.

Ranasta stumbled back, gasping from the sting, before smiling.

Even as the spray of blood splashed the ground, her flesh knit itself back together in seconds. His blow should've disembowelled her.

Varity could add a vitality transplant to all the madwoman had snorted. Even the strongest of Leech-Doctors shouldn't be able to ingest so much at once. Ranasta must've taken more than enough to kill herself, but that wouldn't be until the effects wore off and he'd be long dead himself by then.

"Not even a Shamadar can match me." The veins in Ranasta's neck pulsed violently and her bloodshot eyes opened abnormally wide as she cackled.

"No one's immortal," Varity said, maybe more to convince himself.

Ransta laughed all the harder. "You are when you ingest the life-essence of as many others as I have. They perished so I could live forever!"

The abundance of sorcery had eroded her sanity for sure now. Maybe if he just survived long enough against her, he could wait it out until she expired. But no, that could take hours, and he was barely evading her strikes as it was.

Varity was pretty sure he was going to die. Well, he'd lived a more eventful life than most, and at least he'd saved the dragon before his painful end.

Might as well go out with one final show.

He pretended the soldiers baying for his death were actually the audience come to his final stage show before he retired from acting. Ranasta was just the villain of the piece, Varity the fearless hero of course, not the secret coward who'd fled from war as a child.

"Come then, witch. Slay the monster slayer."

Her bared teeth dripped with blood from her bleeding gums, he thought he saw droplets leaking from her eyes too, but then she was on him.

Varity ducked the first swipe, leaped aside from the other, but was forced to parry the third. To his shock, her sidhe steel didn't shatter his own this time, but Ranasta seized his arm with her free hand before he could escape.

She pulled lightly, snapping his arm at the elbow with a crack that filled his throat with burning vomit. His arm hung limply as he darted out of her reach. He ignored the agony of his various wounds and continued to desperately defend against her, until he jumped away from the next strike, only to trip backwards.

He looked round in a daze, realising he'd fallen over a body.

Mevrin, the young dwarf girl stared up at him with eyes that resembled glass. It was a wonder he recognised her, her face was barely held together from the jagged cut splitting down it. She still clutched a round iron shield in her hands, for all the good it had done her. She hadn't made it out. At least she was free now, maybe.

Ranasta brayed another laugh. "You freed her and the other slaves, didn't you? I may have cleaved her face in half, yet her blood is on your hands."

Rage boiled up from his gut, choking him. She was right. Mevrin's death was down to him, just another cadaver to add on the pile. Varity could fill a castle full of corpses he'd created. Soon he'd join them right at the top, but Ranasta would join him.

He staggered to his feet, suffusing the last pebble of moonstone he had.

Varity knew he couldn't overpower his enemy, but he hoped he could outsmart her. It wouldn't be the first time he won only by luck and cheap tricks.

He held his glowing jewel out to his left, spying the spear gripped in the dead hands of a half-eaten soldier lying beneath a scorprarn. Varity made sure Ranasta saw what he attempted. She raised her sword, doubtless intending to slash the spear apart once he launched it toward her. Instead, he raised the spear an inch off the ground before cutting his feint short, pouring his will into the moonstone to seize Mevin's iron shield and fling it at Ranasta with astonishing force.

The shield spun through the air with the speed of a bullet, lodging into Ranasta's throat. Varity was running before the shield slammed into her neck, shearing halfway through the flesh and sticking there. She reached up to wrench the shield away, crumpling the metal with her bare hands, but Varity reached her first, his sword biting into the back of her neck, sawing her head clean off.

Even as her shocked face bounced to the ground, the gaping hole in her neck resealed itself, leaving her body intact, but motionless. The sorcery was still in her bloodstream and her vitality transplant would keep her going a little longer, but beheading was one of the very few ways to destroy what she'd become, and everyone in the courtyard knew it. For good measure, he planted his sword into her skull, piercing the brain.

Varity stepped away from Ranasta's still blinking head, surprised himself that he'd managed to survive.

After several seconds of stunned silence, the soldiers roared as one, hastening to apprehend him. Varity frantically pulled Ranasta's sword from her hand, which offered no resistance. Without the head, she was no more than a flesh statue.

He sprinted toward the stables, every breath like a stab as his ribs scratched his insides. With what little strength he had left, he sliced the splintered pillar he'd crashed into earlier, ducking inside the stables as the wooden contraption collapsed behind him, blocking the soldiers from pursuit.

Only a few grains of metallic dust coated his palm now, the moonstone all used up. He was feeling the side-effects of suffusing the stone now too. But he couldn't fall now, not when he was so close to escape.

The stables were shrouded in shadow now an army of broken wooden beams blocked out the entrance, yet the cavernous chamber was filled with noises. Horses whickered, camels bleated and Scallions screeched. The sound of the building works crashing had disturbed every mount, but it allowed Varity to find the nearest Scallion with ease.

Dominga scientists always came up with bizarre experiments. Only a decade or so ago, they perfected a creature bred out of stallions and velociraptors. The result wasn't pretty, but it was effective. The Scallion tethered in the stable before him was the vague shape of a warhorse, only covered in mottled green and black scales, with a head more reptilian than equine. The Scallions were vicious steeds, known for their snapping jaws but also for their superior speed. The only way Varity was outrunning the soldiers was upon a Scallion. It was already saddled and ready to ride too. The soldiers here probably didn't want to risk getting their fingers chomped off saddling the Scallion each time.

The beast hissed and reared at his approach. Regrettably, Varity didn't have the time to allow the Scallion to become familiar with him. He threw caution to the winds and skirted round the beast, leaping atop its saddle and holding on for dear life as it writhed.

He murmured calming words in awkward fashion, using his good arm to slice the leather bonds holding the Scallion in its stable. The Scallion stopped fighting him immediately, lurching out of the stable and allowing him to steer it to the single crack of light at the end of the chamber.

He'd gambled on the stable having a back entrance and could've whooped in relief as the Scallion thundered through the wooden door left ajar. The outer wall ringing the castle was only metres away. Varity could hear voiced on the wind, but any soldiers making the long way around the stables weren't yet in sight.

Two soldiers, who must've been on watch, manned the small side gate set in the outer wall. They sprang into action as Varity and his Scallion ripped across the sands toward them.

Varity swung at the orcish soldier on his left, the butt of his sword slamming against his helm, knocking him out. The dusk elf guard was less fortunate, as he whirled, spear raised, the Scallion shot forward like a striking snake, giant

jaws locking down on the elf's head and crunching tight,

triggering a red mist.

Making sure never to get close to his mount's mouth,

Varity spurred the Scallion through the side gate and away

into the deserts.

*

Dominga soldiers followed him for two days across the

endless sands. Preventing them from getting any mounts to

follow after him had slowed the soldiers considerably.

They were but shiny dots on the horizon by the time he'd

ridden miles away.

Still, the blighters were persistent and who knew how

long they would've tailed him if he hadn't reached

Masqera. The plains of smooth sand erupted into giant

dunes, who in turn were dwarfed by the white stone

pyramid, Masqera; the last bastion of an extinct civilisation. Varity left his Scallion by the pyramid's entrance, hoping his hunters would think he'd hidden inside the supposedly haunted ruins.

He then skirted around the pyramid and entered the network of caves nestled behind it. He used his onyx jewel to cause an avalanche and block the mouth of the cave he entered.

Inside the cave, he recovered the supplies he'd stashed there shortly after taking on this job, gleefully draining his waterskin for the first time in two days and consuming food for the first time in a week. Fortunately, he didn't need to eat as regularly as the human he'd once been, but he still enjoyed it. Shamadar didn't need as much sleep as a human either, except for times when they were badly injured, like now. His arm and ribs no longer felt broken, but they wouldn't heal properly until he had a few hours rest.

*

The home of the Dragonshade tribe appeared on the horizon on the third day. It was hard to miss. From afar, he saw the corpse of the Elder Beast in all its glory.

Millenia ago, creatures roamed Serathur with the size and strength to topple cities in their wake. Fortunately, all that remained of them now were their bones and their frozen corpses.

This ancient monster, large as a castle, closest resembled a turtle crossed with a horned beetle, yet its eight legs ended in talons. It's great shell, perhaps once scaled, appeared made of stone now, and Varity thought he saw a shape stir high atop the shell, out of sight.

Varity struggled against the heat, and the sheer distance he travelled on foot. He'd long since drained the last of his water, but he'd known Dragonshade wasn't far from the Maqera ruins.

Still, covered in dust, dirt and dried blood, he must've looked a beggar as he walked up to the tribe's village.

The home of the Dragonshade tribe was like most villages in the world, only instead of mud huts or stone houses, the tribespeople lived inside hollow scarabs, under the vast shadow of the dead Elder Beast.

The Cimhuran children saw him first; one young as ten already had his first pale red tattoo. They'd been playing beyond their homes, where the deserts gleamed gold, but scampered back under the shade as Varity neared. The Scallion was likely the cause for alarm. By the time Varity dismounted at the village's outskirts, Dragonshade's three fiercest warriors ran to greet him.

Two of the three women were armed with blowpipes-he dreaded to know what poison the darts were doused in-whilst the third, Arassa, lowered her scythe in realisation.

"You live, Varati." Arassa's accent was so naturally clipped, he was unsure if she was happy or angry to see him.

"It's pronounced Varity. I-" He broke off as a sudden roar split the sky, momentarily deafening him.

He tensed, arms straining on his Scallion's reins to keep the animal from bolting. Though it seemed Eshindra's roar wasn't one of threat, as the next sound hailing from the shell of the Beast high above was a sleepy groan.

"I see Eshindra beat me here."

"Yesterday, she returns," said Arassa, a smile blooming across her face and melting the fierce mask. "Our celebrations lasted all night. You have given us our goddess back."

Varity grinned back. "Aye, the jobs I'm used to commonly revolve around killing monsters who are terrorising innocents, it was a nice change to set a creature free."

The rest of the tribe stood outside their scarab huts, watching him. The younger of them watched him in curiosity and awe, the elders with gratitude and even a few smiles, whilst a handful of others gazed at him with the same distrust they'd had when he accepted their task. One elderly man sat across from a young boy, a scorpion the size of a hound between them. From what Varity could see, the man was using the scorpion's blood to tattoo the boy.

"I confess, when we asked a strange warrior for aid, we did not truly think you'd succeed," Arassa said, the two women beside her nodding agreement. "It is a miracle."

"No miracles, just talent.' He lied, knowing he'd had more than a touch of luck too.

"These metal men caught Eshindra whilst hunting, we think," said Arassa. "We've never seen the metal men come close to Dragonshade. They have not come this far into Cimhura."

"Good, so the Dominga won't capture her again. Though I think she'll be ready for them if they try."

"As will we, we will fight like many tribes are already. Our elders wanted peace, but since the metal men stole our idol, we will join the seven tribes and fight for our home."

Varity didn't have the heart to tell them it was fruitless. The Dominga had slowly conquered every other country in the continent, Cimhura was just the last.

"So, I held up my end of the bargain. I trust you shall honour yours too."

Arassa gestured behind her, beckoning forward a tiny old lady, whose mass of tattoos looked like they had wrinkles. She held a small chest in her wizened hands, yet tottered as if the weight of it was about to cause her to topple.

Varity gently took it from her hands, opening the lid and grinning at the chest's contents. Perhaps four dozen jewels, all manner of hues, glistened within the chest. A fitting reward for the dangers he'd faced. He could sell all the jewels he couldn't suffuse himself, yet Varity would've done more to get these treasures. He'd live like a king for years, or likely months with his spending habits. He didn't know where the tribe had gleaned such a bounty, nor did he care.

"Where will you go now?" Arassa asked.

"It's best I lay low for a while; a whole other continent seems wisest. I recently heard about a little job across the sea."

A loud snuffling made him look up and see a strange face staring back at him, peeking over the rim of the Elder Beast's shell.

He smiled up at the baby dragon. He often felt a strange melancholy after completing a contract. Even if he'd slain the thing terrorising a village and its people, he took no joy in killing the cruellest of monsters. But saving Eshindra, so she could return to her child, that made him feel good for once.

*

Varity strolled down the spine-train, surrounded by opulence and the thunderous clatter of wheels. The metal at his feet vibrated and the train itself seemed to purr. He could see the ocean metres away through the windows either side of him. Surreal didn't start to describe it.

Those giant metal snakes they called trains were only a few years old themselves, but at least they travelled on the ground, not across the spine of a long dead leviathan. The Elder Beast's skeleton was so vast its head actually lay on Morinthia, whilst its tail reached Cimhura. The trolladin engineers, known for their mad inventions, had gotten the idea of building train tracks along the spine that connected the continents.

Not only was being inside the train contraption unnerving, but buying a ticket had been ludicrously expensive. Varity had sold his stolen Scallion to a mercenary on the road, once he'd ridden three days away from the Dragonshade village and back to civilisation. He'd had to use all the Crescents his Scallion got him to get a ride on this death-trap.

He stopped in the corridor between compartments as the voices in one piqued his interest.

"Yes, Arch Duke Ferdinez has said he'll reward the Tusk of Oron itself to whatever warrior can slay the beast plaguing his lands."

Varity casually strode inside the compartment as the gentlemen finished speaking. He shared the train-car with another refined gentleman and two ladies dressed in bonnets and ballgowns. All four of them were Palaesian, a kingdom that seemed to run on snobbery.

"No, waiter, we've already eaten?" One of the gentlemen waved Varity away, the very feather in his cap fluttering with indignation.

"You mistake me, sir." Varity needlessly straightened his coat, still splattered with dried bloodstains, and sat down between the two women.

The quartet's irritated expressions turned to awe as they actually looked at him, noticing the black rim around his eyes.

"A Shamadar!" The lady with a fan waved it ever more aggressively in front of her face. "All manner of rogues and ruffians are said to be clamouring to Morinthia to slay this new, terrifying beast. How did you hear about it?"

"A dear Mereshi friend of mine gave me a tip." Varity plucked the cigarillo from one of the gentleman's hands and helped himself to a drag.

He lounged back in his seat, heedless of the looks on all their faces. "So, tell me, what monster does this Arch Duke need killing, and how much is he paying?"

THE END

Find the Sequel to Deathrunes and Dragons here:

Under A Torn Moon

Book Two in the Songs of Serathur

https://www.amazon.com/dp/B09MNVHC

RB

https://www.amazon.co.uk/dp/B09MNVH

CRB

Under A Torn Moon Teaser...

Vyrella mutilated herself once more, she was used to it now. Fear thundered through her mind, yet she kept her expression bereft of both fright and pain. Though she knew how to carve her skin in ways to render the least amount of scarring, the sting was still sharp.

Vyrella thought the knife might slip from the sweat dripping through her fingers, but she kept a steady hand as she gouged the eight-pointed rune into her palm. At once, beads of crimson welled through the ridges she'd wrought. Her flesh, whiter than snow, made the fluid resemble crushed cherries. The glyph flashed gold once she'd joined the last line. Vyrella frantically dropped to her knees, pressing her bloody palm in the centre of one stone tile. Her blood smeared in a poor imitation of the rune, but it should be enough. Her hair, pale as bone, was so long it threatened to spill across the floor and smudge the blood. She hastily seized her hair and pulled it behind her shoulders.

Stupid. She should've brought a cord to tie it back before the trial began. She'd come prepared as she could be. Nine knives nestled within her suit of manticore leather, and she'd conserved her sorcery for three days. The grandmages forbade any use of her poisons, however. If she could only utilise the artefacts from her former career, Vyrella's heart would've beat in a less frantic rhythm right now.

"Ten seconds elapsed," Ob'chara cried, his mandible clicks echoing around the silent hall. "Ten more to go."

She glanced instinctively at the grandmaster in the gallery above. Ob'chara's appearance was eerie even as the ghunlin race went. His compound eyes appeared like polished copper plates as they bored into her, his antennae listing above his ant-like head. His body was human, if almost skeletal and covered in a thin coating of amber.

Her fellow mages also watched her from the gallery, leaning over the railings and forming a mass ring which encircled what would be Vyrella's battlefield. Many of her peers disguised their eagerness to watch her fail and die, whilst others let their excitement show. *How many desire to witness my body torn limb for limb?* Some would want her to survive—surely.

How many trials have I observed? How many fellow Acolytes have I seen fail in this hall?

Fortunately, most of the mages were hard to discern in the blue gloom that suffused the room. Both the tiles at her feet and the walls were flawless cobalt. The cavernous hall was lit only by twisted candles, wax long warped as sweat dripped off them in rivulets.

Shrin, her only friend in this cursed pyramid, was serving time in the isolation cells. Otherwise, Shrin would be at least one friendly face. *Maybe it's better this way.* If Vyrella failed, at least Shrin wouldn't have to watch helplessly as she was mauled and eaten alive.

The spectators were supposed to be silent, but several snickers rustled amidst the crowd and one murmur sounded like someone making a bet on how quickly Vyrella would perish.

"The ice elf doesn't stand a chance," someone shouted suddenly.

Vyrella drove her contemporaries from her mind, she should care naught whether they wanted her to succeed. Ob'Chara was the only one who counted. He was the only one she needed to impress. Even surviving might not be enough if the grandmaster deemed it.

With her first rune done, she switched the knife between her hands, carving the next glyph into her other palm, heedless of the blood leaking freely across its handle.

As part of the trial, no mage could know what manner of monster they'd face, but Vyrella had concocted a plan that should work for anything. As a Flesh-Artist, Ob'Chara permitted her a scant period of time to prepare, since her method of magery was often the slowest. Yet twenty seconds still might not be enough.

She felt her chest heaving, breath billowing, as she scrawled the seven-sided spiral into her palm, leaving the very last lines half an inch from connecting. She couldn't trigger the spell yet, not until she knew with absolute certainty it would connect.

"Time passed!" Ob'Chara cried. "Bring the beast forth."